PATRIOTIC SYMBOLS

The Bald Eagle

Nancy Harris

Heinemann Library
Chicago, Illinois

© 2008 Heinemann Library
a division of Reed Elsevier Inc.
Chicago, Illinois

Customer Service **888-454-2279**

Visit our Web site at **www.heinemannlibrary.com**

All rights reserved. No part of this publication may be reproduced or transmitted in any form or by or by any means, electronic or mechanical, including photocopying, recording, taping, or any information storage and retrieval system, without permission in writing from the publisher.

Photo Research by Tracy Cummins and Tracey Engel
Designed by Kimberly R. Miracle
Maps by Mapping Specialists, Ltd.
Printed and bound in China by South China Printing Company

10 09
10 9 8 7 6 5 4 3 2

10 Digit ISBN: 1-4034-9380-4 (hc)   1-4034-9387-1 (pb)

Library of Congress Cataloging-in-Publication Data
Harris, Nancy, 1956-
  The bald eagle / Nancy Harris.
    p. cm. -- (Patriotic symbols)
  Includes bibliographical references and index.
  ISBN-13: 978-1-4034-9380-4 (hc)
  ISBN-13: 978-1-4034-9387-3 (pb)
 1. United States--Seal--Juvenile literature. 2. Bald eagle--United States--Juvenile literature. 3. Emblems, National--United States--Juvenile literature. 4. Animals--Symbolic aspects--Juvenile literature. 5. Signs and symbols--United States--Juvenile literature. I. Title.
  CD5610.H27 2007
  929.90973--dc22
                        2006039383

Acknowledgements
The author and publisher are grateful to the following for permission to reproduce copyright material: ©AP Photo **pp. 17** (Gene J. Puskar), **23** (Koji Sasahara); ©Corbis **pp. 5** (flag, Royalty Free), **8** (Brooks Kraft), **14** (Bettmann), **16** (Joseph Sohm; Visions of America), **21** (Ariel Skelley), **22** (Royalty Free), **23** (Brooks Kraft); ©Getty Images **pp. 4** (Don Farrall), **9** (Gary Vestal), **23** (Don Farrall); ©istockphoto **p. 5** (Liberty Bell, drbueller); ©North Wind Picture Archives **pp. 12, 13, 20**; ©PhotoEdit **p. 6** (Eric Fowke); ©Shutterstock **pp. 5** (Statue of Liberty, Ilja Mašík), **5** (White House, Uli); ©SuperStock **pp. 10** (Richard Cummins), **18** (Brand X).

Cover image reproduced courtesy of The White House. Back cover image reproduced with permission of ©SuperStock (Brand X).

Every effort has been made to contact copyright holders of any material reproduces in this book. Any omissions will be rectified in subsequent printings if notice is given to the publisher.

Contents

What Is a Symbol? 4
The Bald Eagle Seal. 6
Words 10
Colonies. 12
Olive Branch 16
13 Arrows 18
What It Tells You 20
Bald Eagle Facts 22
Timeline. 22
Picture Glossary. 23
Index. 24

What Is a Symbol?

The Bald Eagle Seal is a symbol.
A symbol is a type of sign.

A symbol shows you something.
A symbol can have words.

The Bald Eagle Seal

The Bald Eagle Seal is a special symbol.

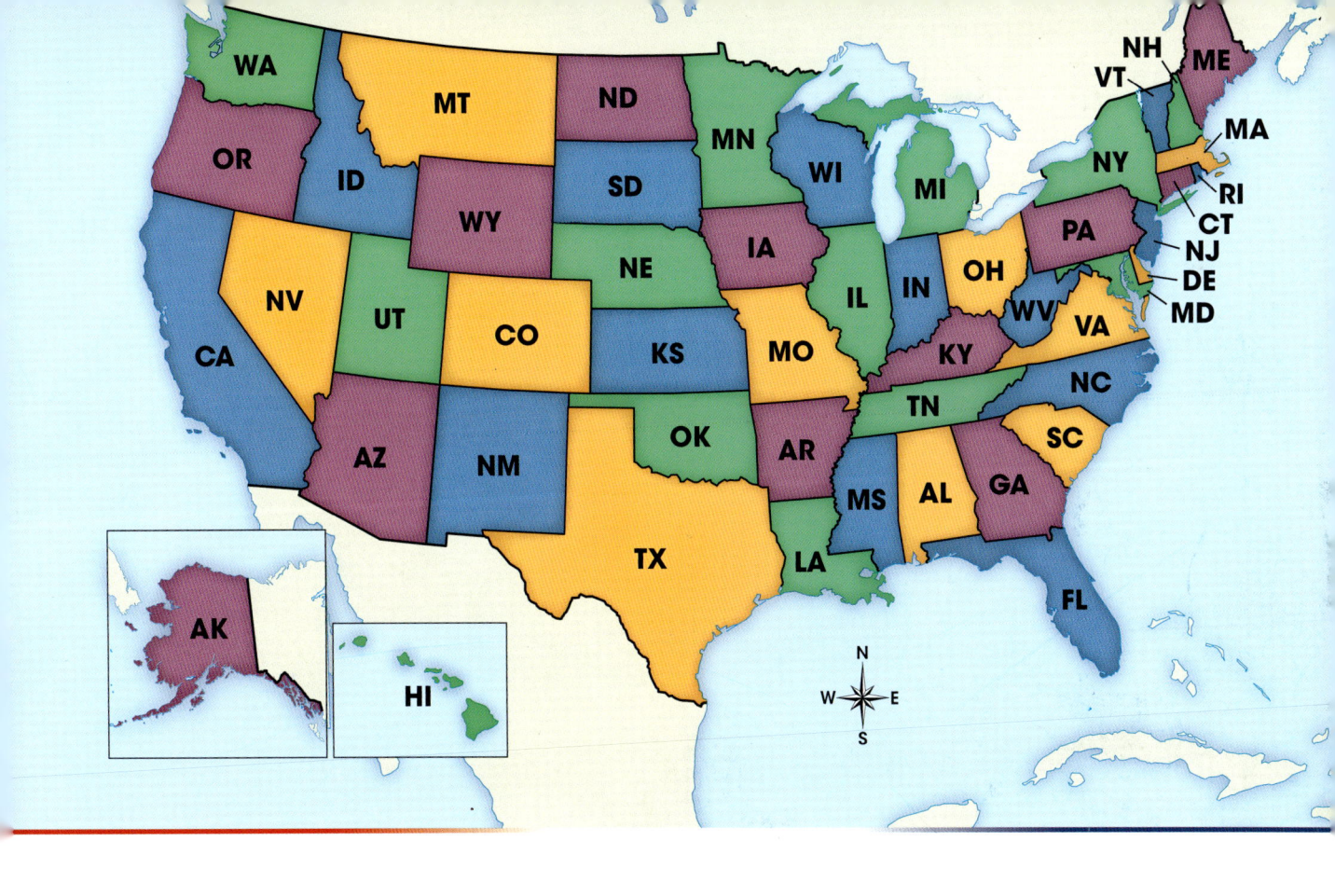

It is a symbol of the United States of America.
The United States of America is a country.

The Bald Eagle Seal is a patriotic symbol.

It shows the beliefs of the United States.
The bald eagle flying is a symbol of freedom.

Words

The Bald Eagle Seal has special words on it.

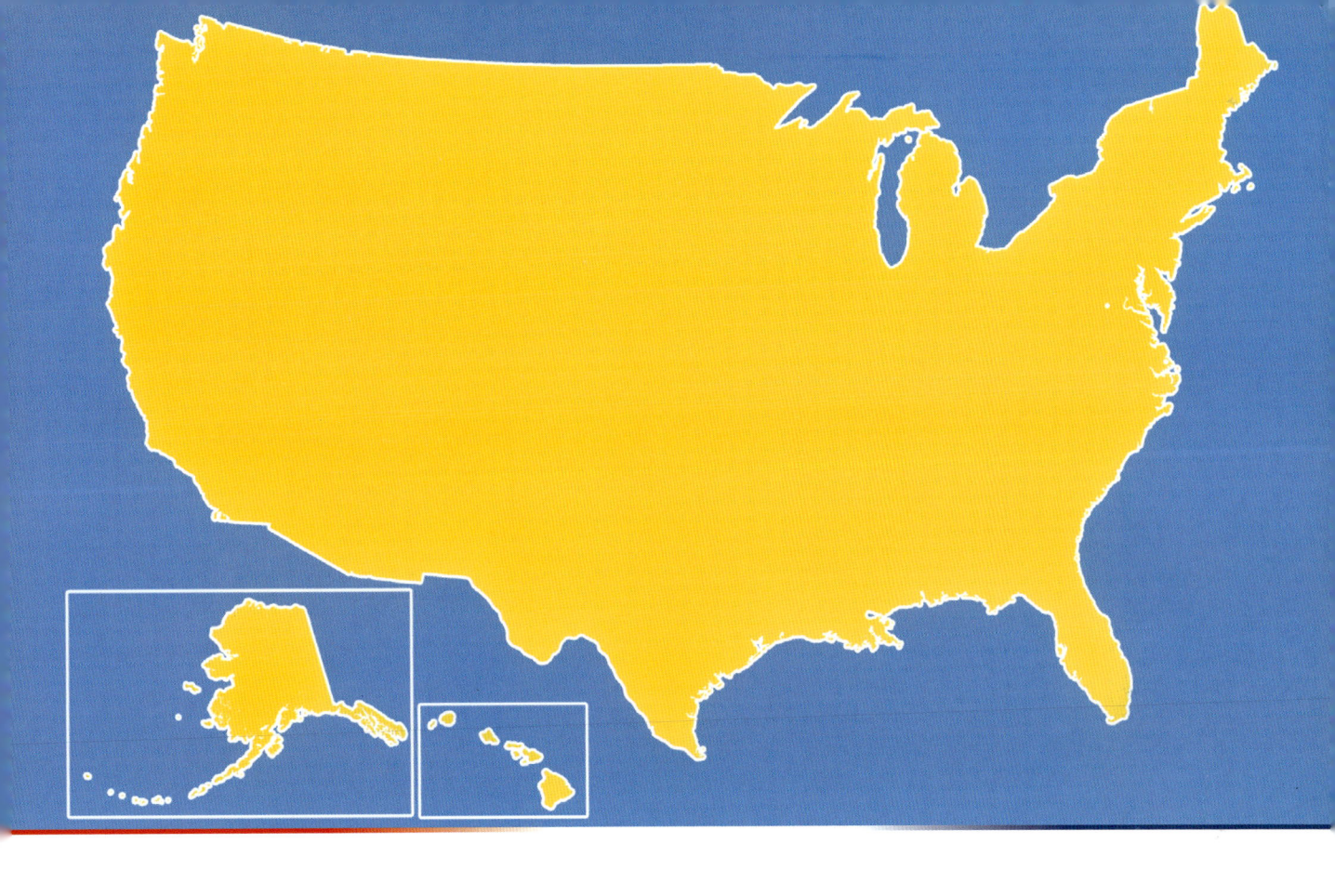

The words mean, *out of many, one.*

Colonies

The word *many* is a symbol of the 13 colonies. A colony is a place ruled by another country.

People moved to the colonies from other countries.

13

These people fought to create a free country.

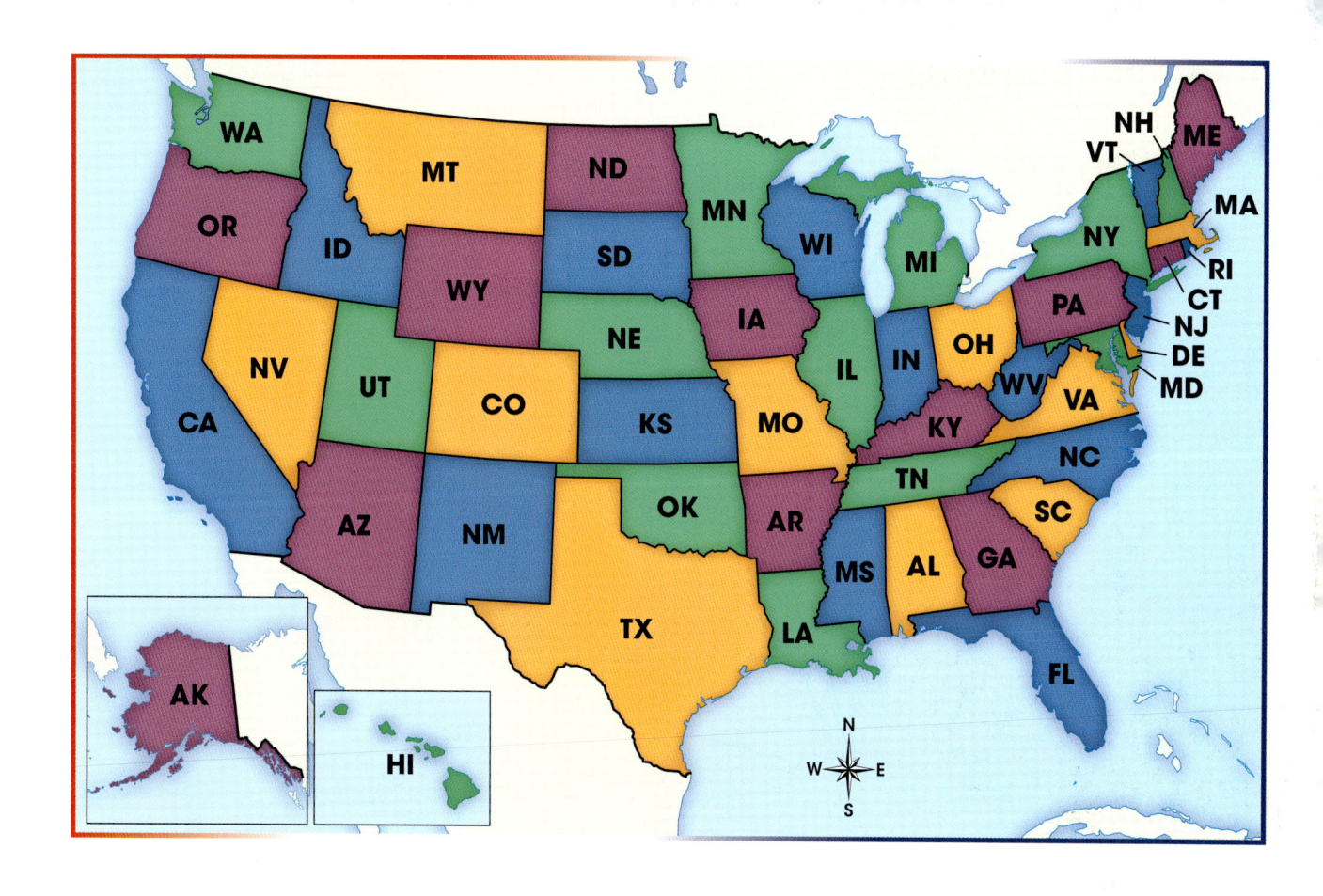

The word *one* is a symbol of the free country. The country is the United States of America.

15

Olive Branch

olive branch

The bald eagle holds an olive branch.

The olive branch is a symbol of peace.

13 Arrows

arrows

The bald eagle holds 13 arrows.

The First 13 States

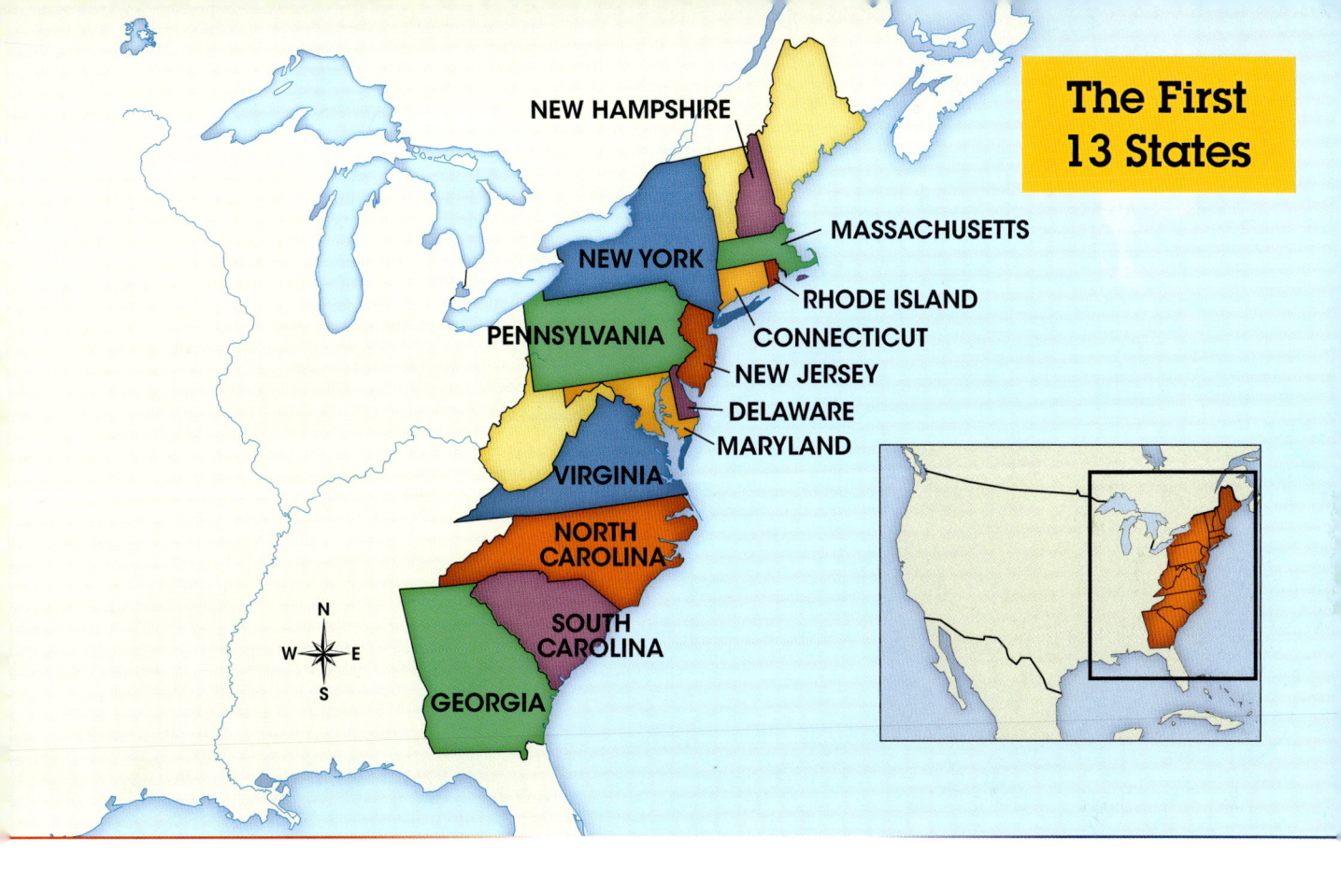

- NEW HAMPSHIRE
- MASSACHUSETTS
- NEW YORK
- RHODE ISLAND
- CONNECTICUT
- PENNSYLVANIA
- NEW JERSEY
- DELAWARE
- MARYLAND
- VIRGINIA
- NORTH CAROLINA
- SOUTH CAROLINA
- GEORGIA

The arrows are a symbol of the first 13 states.

19

What It Tells You

The Bald Eagle Seal honors the beginning of the United States.

The Seal is a symbol of a free country.

Bald Eagle Facts

★ Bald eagles have a wingspan that is six to seven feet wide.

★ Bald eagles only live in North America.

Timeline

1700 1750 1782 1800

✪ The Bald Eagle Seal was made in 1782.

Picture Glossary

country an area of land that is ruled by the same leader

patriotic believing in your country

seal a stamp that stands for something

symbol something that stands for something else. Symbols can stand for feelings, places, or objects.

23

Index

arrow, 18-19
colony, 12-13
country, 7, 12-15, 21
freedom, 9
olive branch, 16-17
patriotic, 8
state, 19
United States of America, 7, 9, 15, 20

Note to Parents and Teachers

The study of patriotic symbols introduces young readers to our country's government and history. Books in this series begin by defining a symbol before focusing on the history and significance of a specific patriotic symbol. Use the timeline and facts section on page 22 to introduce readers to these non-fiction features.

The text has been carefully chosen with the advice of a literacy expert to enable beginning readers success while reading independently or with moderate support. An expert in the field of early childhood social studies curriculum was consulted to provide interesting and appropriate content.

You can support children's nonfiction literacy skills by helping students use the table of contents, headings, picture glossary, and index.